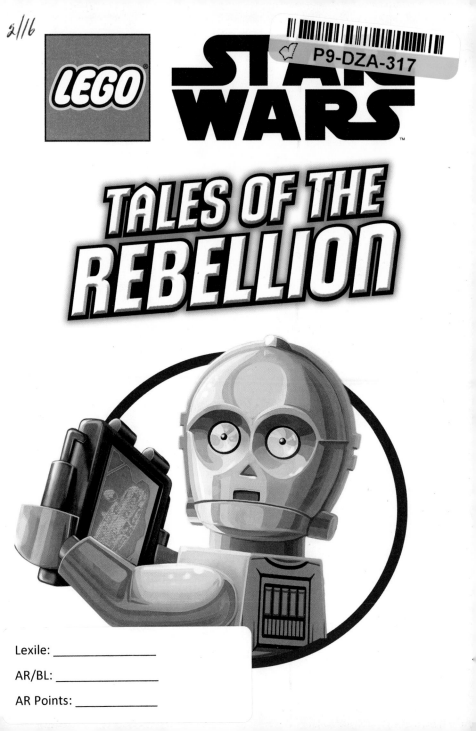

LEGO® STAR WARS™

TALES OF THE REBELLION

Lexile: _____

AR/BL: _____

AR Points: _____

"Catch That Jedi", "Operation: Later Vader", and "A Most Dangerous Droid" written by Ace Landers

Illustrated by Ameet Studio

LEGO, the LEGO logo, the Brick and Knob configurations and the Minifigure are trademarks of the LEGO Group. © 2016 The LEGO Group. Produced by Scholastic Inc. under license from The LEGO Group.

© & ™ 2016 LUCASFILM LTD. Used Under Authorization.

ISBN 978-0-545-87326-0

10 9 8 7 6 5 4 3 2 1   16 17 18 19 20

Printed in the U.S.A.   40
This edition first Scholastic printing 2016

Book design by Ameet Studio

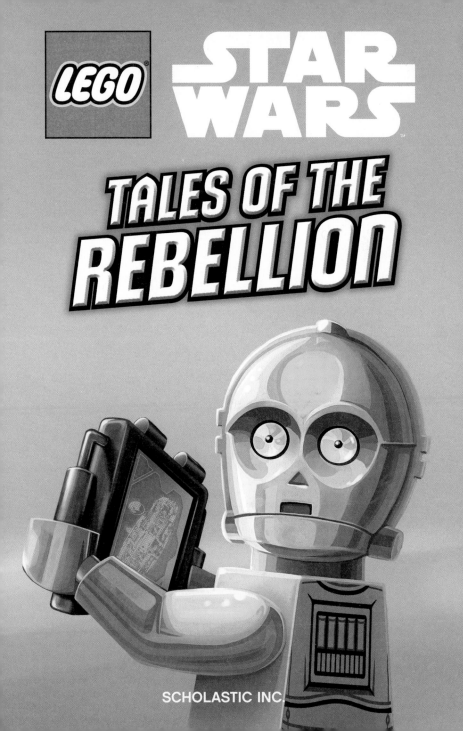

LEGO® STAR WARS™

TALES OF THE REBELLION

SCHOLASTIC INC.

CONTENTS

WHAT YOU SHOULD KNOW ABOUT THE REBELS AND THEIR MISSIONS

Hello! My name is C-3PO, and I am a protocol droid. My fragile circuits have always preferred peace and quiet, but somehow I managed to get involved in all this rebel ruckus! So let me begin by setting the scene and telling you what's been going on. As long as there's nobody shooting nearby, that is . . .

A long time ago, an evil Emperor took control of the galaxy. Those were dark times, but the more the Emperor tightened his grip, the more star systems slipped through his fingers. The rebels who opposed the Empire's reign were scattered into many small groups across the whole galaxy. This helped them hide and carry out their missions in secret.

THE BRAVE CREW

Ever since the Rebellion began, the rebels have had to keep changing bases to remain undetected. First, it was Yavin, then Hoth—my screws are getting loose from all the moving! If only I could operate in a nice, calm droid office, far away from all this adventure . . .

I have no complaints about the *Millennium Falcon* crew, however. They are the most amazing group I have ever met, if my memory chip serves me right.

First, there's Master Luke, who is training to become a Jedi Knight; then the brave and beautiful Princess Leia, who turned out to be Master Luke's sister; the space pirate and rogue Han Solo; and the furry co-pilot and mechanic, Chewbacca. For all of these heroes, messing with Imperial lackeys soon became their favorite hobby!

THE FIRST VICTORY

The rebels' first big mission was finding the Death Star. Nobody expected them to destroy it. Especially not the Death Star's crew . . . you should have seen the look on their faces! Anyway, the united fleet of the Rebellion achieved its first great success.

Blasting the battle station would have been impossible without the final shot fired by Luke Skywalker, the young Jedi pilot. He almost didn't make it, with the terrifying Darth Vader flying hot on his tail—oh, dear! Suddenly, Han Solo came to his rescue in the *Millennium Falcon*, and damaged Vader's ship, which spun away like a Twi'lek ballerina in some unknown direction. I cheered so hard my vocalizer almost fell off! And for a while, everybody forgot about the dreadful Lord Vader.

THE FINAL BATTLE

But then, the Emperor decided to start building a second Death Star, and we knew all jokes were over. The rebels had to strike first, before it was completed. Personally, I'd rather have stayed on the other side of the galaxy, but this time I found myself right in the center of the action.

The action was on a forest moon of the planet Endor, where I was supposed to assist a rebel commando in turning off the battle station's force field. Our mission was a success. We foiled the Emperor's evil plans and destroyed the Empire.

Oh, dear, dear. Those were turbulent days . . . but glorious, too.

Now, read some more stories about my friends, the rebels, and their adventures fighting against the Empire and its evil dark leaders . . .

CATCH THAT JEDI

During downtime between missions, the crew of the *Ghost* landed at a cargo station on Lothal that was supposed to be off the beaten path of the Empire.

Hera, the captain of the *Ghost*, convinced everyone it was safe. "Trust me, there's no way the Inquisitor would look for us here!"

"Just like the time you told us it was easy to sleep

in zero gravity?" asked Zeb.

"Or the time you told us Chopper knew how to cook?" asked Sabine.

"Hey, I liked Chopper's cooking," admitted Ezra. "It had a lot of iron . . . and nuts . . . and bolts."

"If Hera says we're staying here for the day, then we're staying here," confirmed Kanan. "End of discussion."

As the Jedi started to go back to his room, Ezra made a suggestion. "Since we have the time, Kanan, could we spend the day doing some Jedi training?"

"Sure, but not here. Let's see what kind of trouble we can find outside."

First they practiced levitation concentration. Kanan showed the young apprentice how to lift crates.

"You need to focus."

But when it was Ezra's turn, focusing was not his strongest skill. *Clunk!* He dropped the crate, and it cracked open, releasing hundreds of bouncing balls. "Oh, boy! I am such a Jedi butterfingers!"

"Technically, you're a *Padawan* butterfingers," corrected Kanan. But the balls gave him an idea. "What if we made this into a game? Use the Force to try to hit me with the balls. If you get me, you win. But if you miss me, then I win."

Quickly, Ezra tried to hurl the balls at Kanan, but the Jedi dodged each throw.

"This is impossible!" cried Ezra. "If these can't catch you, then maybe I can!" He lunged at Kanan, but the Jedi swiftly stepped aside.

"Looks like someone wants to play Jedi Tag!" said Kanan. "You're it!"

With that, Kanan leapt up and took off, running through the cargo station. Ezra followed in hot pursuit.

Moving swiftly, Ezra knew that a Jedi must be

ready for anything, but he wasn't ready for a loth-cat attack!

The furry feline made Ezra trip and fall headfirst into a crate of Jawa robes. "Bad kitty!" he exclaimed. But the loth-cat snapped at him again, causing the young rebel to stumble backward through a doorway into a room where a dangerous conversation was taking place.

"Grand Moff, to what do I owe this dishonor?" It was the Inquisitor! And he was talking to a hologram of the evil leader, Wilhuff Tarkin.

"Have you found the rogue Jedi yet?"

"Not yet, but something tells me Kanan's close . . . closer than we think."

Ezra tried to tiptoe away, but the Inquisitor heard him. "You there—halt!"

What else could Ezra do? He draped a Jawa robe over his shoulders and said, "Utinni?"

The Inquisitor looked suspicious, but then again, he always looked suspicious. "Aren't you a little big for a Jawa?"

"Yeah, but you're a little clueless for a bad guy!" called Kanan from behind him.

The Inquisitor tried to draw his lightsaber, but Ezra threw the Jawa robe in his face, then ran away with Kanan. The Inquisitor turned to follow them, but the Grand Moff's hologram appeared again.

"Did you get him yet?" asked Tarkin.

"Soon enough!" shouted the Inquisitor as he began the chase.

For Ezra and Kanan, the game had changed

from Catch That Jedi to Escape the Dark Side. They jumped through room after room again, but this time Kanan Force-pushed a box that smashed into the Inquisitor. It was filled with dainty tiaras.

"Princesses! I hate princesses!" screamed the Inquisitor.

Tarkin rang again. "One other thing, Inquisitor, remember . . . *Hmm*, I'm sorry, pretty little princess. I must have dialed the wrong hologram number."

"It's me!" shouted the Inquisitor, who was wearing the tiaras. "Now, with all due respect, don't call me, I'll call you!"

Tired of playing games, the Inquisitor leapt in a different direction.

"Ha!" said Ezra. "That dark side dolt is running away! I think we won!"

"Don't celebrate yet, kid," said Kanan. The Jedi was crouched and on the lookout when the Inquisitor attacked with his lightsaber. Kanan barely had time to push Ezra out of the way. Luckily, he landed in a pile of balls.

Kanan drew his lightsaber and a great duel erupted. The Inquisitor slashed while Kanan parried, trying to defend himself.

"It's over now, Jedi," bellowed the Inquisitor. But just as he seemed to have Kanan beat, the Grand Moff's hologram appeared again.

"Now, where was I? We must have had a bad connection last time. Ah, yes, scorching the Jedi from the galaxy . . ."

Kanan used the distraction to kick the Inquisitor off him. "Now, Ezra!"

Then, with the Force, Ezra levitated all the balls and threw them at the Inquisitor. He destroyed the first few with his lightsaber, but there were too many bouncing around in every direction. Soon the Inquisitor was buried under a giant, colorful pile.

"I've trained you well," said Kanan.

"Yeah, at dodgeball, but that's not going to beat the Empire," admitted Ezra. "So let's get out of here before the rest of the Empire wants in on the game."

The two rebels dashed back to the *Ghost* and escaped to fight another day.

OPERATION: LATER VADER

Having just destroyed the first Death Star, the rebels celebrated their biggest victory yet against the Empire. Princess Leia even awarded medals to Han Solo and Luke Skywalker for their bravery in the battle.

Later that day, Han and Luke were retelling their glory story to a bunch of new recruits in the rebel cafeteria. Chewbacca, on the other hand, was wolfing down as much ice cream as possible from the all-you-can-eat ice cream celebration.

"And then we jumped into the garbage!" Luke laughed. "Talk about some stinky ideas."

"To be fair, I told you that I had a bad feeling about that place," admitted Han.

"Of course you did," said Leia. "It was the Death Star! Everyone had a bad feeling about that place."

All the rebels laughed—all except the giant Wookiee who sat in the corner and seemed to be in a bad mood. Chewbacca stood up and started waving his arms to interrupt Han and Luke's story time.

"How come you're not laughing it up, fuzzball?" asked Han. "Can't you see I'm trying to share my adventures over here?"

"Yeah, Chewie," agreed Princess Leia. "It's not every day that you blow up the Empire."

Chewbacca pointed to his mouth and tried to say something, but no sound came out.

"Oh, no, Chewie!" groaned Luke. "You ate too much ice cream, didn't you? He's completely frozen his voice!"

"Is there another way you can tell us what's on your mind?" asked Han.

The Wookiee quickly grabbed a tablecloth and draped it over himself. Then he placed a bowl upside down on his head and used a fork to make himself look like Darth Vader.

"Well, I'll be a wampa's uncle," said Han. "Chewie's right. We blew up the Death Star, but we also let Darth Vader escape!"

"Wait, you mean we didn't win yet?" asked Luke Skywalker. "I thought that was it? One and done."

But the Rebel Alliance knew that as long as Darth Vader was still free in the world, no one was safe. They decided to capture him. Han Solo, Luke Skywalker,

Chewbacca, and Princess Leia all boarded the *Millennium Falcon* and blasted back to where the Death Star used to be.

There was debris everywhere. But Han was an excellent pilot and dodged the leftover Death Star scraps.

"By my guess, Vader should have flown in that direction after you forced him off course," said Leia. She pointed to a cluster of stars.

"How do you know?" asked Luke.

"Princess intuition," said Leia.

But then Chewie picked up a signal on the radar. Lots of signals to be exact. He pointed out the hundreds of blips on the screen.

"You're right," said Han. "It looks like we're not the only ones looking for Vader. Space is crawling with TIE fighters."

Luke frowned nervously. "Maybe we should turn

back? Usually Obi-Wan tells me all sorts of awesome things when I'm going into a really bad situation. Like, *Use the Force, Luke*, or *Great shot, kid, that was one in a million*."

"Hey, I said that," complained Han Solo.

"But this time Obi-Wan is totally quiet. It's almost like he's saying," Luke continued in a fake ghostly voice, *"Luke, go home . . . and don't worry about Darth Vader. You'll probably never see him again."*

Then Obi-Wan's real voice echoed through Luke's head. *"I said no such thing! And quit making fun of my ghostly voice!"*

"Well, that settles it," said Leia. "What's our plan of attack?"

"Looks like it's time for more diversionary tactics!" said Han.

"Aw, does this mean we have to hide again?" asked Luke.

"Nope," said Han. "I've still got a few tricks up my sleeve. Chewie, let's get sneaky!"

Outside the *Millennium Falcon*, legions of stormtroopers in TIE fighters were also combing through the space wreckage in search of their missing leader.

Suddenly, a new, larger TIE fighter entered the search. It was the *Millennium Falcon* in disguise!

"Hah!" cried Han. "Now nobody knows it's us!"

But then the other TIE fighters surrounded their ship. "Let us see your identification," demanded one of the stormtroopers.

"Um, you don't need to see our identification?" tried Luke.

"Um, yes, we do," answered the stormtrooper. "You don't look at all like one of the Empire's fleet. Hold on . . . were you trying to use the Force on us?"

"Move along, Han!" Luke panicked, and Han

blasted into hyperspace to escape.

"Okay, you guys," said Leia. "We've tried things your way. Now we're going to try my way."

So the *Millennium Falcon* returned, but this time in a clever, new costume. It was disguised as an Imperial Dry Cleaning Delivery Service. "Everyone loves the cleaning crew," said Leia.

"Yay! Finally! Clean clothes!" cheered the entire TIE fighter force. "Let them through!"

"See," said Leia. "Now, Luke, go collect all the dirty stormtrooper uniforms. Then we can go nab that no-good Sith."

As the Imperial Dry Cleaning Delivery Service passed through the TIE fighter checkpoints collecting uniforms, another starship followed the rebels.

"I have a weird feeling that we're being followed," said Luke.

"Not a chance," said Han.

Chewbacca slapped his head in frustration. Using spare parts from the cockpit, he dressed himself like a

DRY CLEANING DELIVERY SERVICE

very unfriendly bounty hunter.

"Oh, no," moaned Han. It turned out that Darth Vader wasn't the only person in the galaxy who was being hunted. Boba Fett had been hot on Han's trail ever since they left Yavin 4!

"I bet you're really good at charades, Chewie," commented Luke.

Suddenly, an explosion rocked the *Millennium Falcon*. Boba Fett was attacking! Han swerved into an asteroid field to try to get away from the bounty hunter's ship, *Slave I*. But Boba Fett was also an amazing pilot. He zoomed around the asteroids

effortlessly. Luke ran to the blasters and blew up one of the space boulders next to the bounty hunter, but Fett was ready. He steered safely past every chunk.

Then Han drove into a cave. "He'll never find us in here."

"Han, don't you think this cave looks a bit strange?" asked Leia nervously.

"I don't know," said Han. "All these dark caves with giant teeth look alike to me."

"Did you say *GIANT TEETH*?!" shouted Luke.

Suddenly, they realized the *Millennium Falcon* was trapped inside a giant space worm.

"What are we going to do now?" asked Han frantically.

But Chewbacca already had an answer. With the push of a button, the *Millennium Falcon* dumped all of the dirty stormtrooper laundry into the mouth of the monster.

"YUCK!" bellowed the beast as it spit everything out, including the *Falcon*! Han kicked it into high gear and blasted past Boba Fett.

"Looks like we made a clean, er, dirty getaway!" said Luke. "But your friend is still right behind us."

"This guy is like C-3PO and R2-D2," said Han. "We just can't seem to get rid of him!"

"Try turning here!" said Leia as they approached a mysterious flying object.

Han veered the spaceship and couldn't believe his eyes. It was Darth Vader's broken TIE fighter. The rebels had found him!

Luke turned on the radio and the crew instantly heard Vader's terrifying—and terrified—voice.

"Hello? Hello? Anyone? Ugh, I'll never hear the end of this from the Emperor. What kind of a Sith Lord gets lost in space? And why did I paint my TIE fighter black when so many other TIE fighters are grayish-white? Great thinking, Vader. Because black is the easiest color to see in space . . . oh, wait a minute . . . no, it's not!"

The sight of Vader took Boba Fett by surprise, which allowed Han to blast *Slave I*. Suddenly, Boba

Fett found himself bouncing back into the asteroid field. It was like he was trapped in a pinball machine.

Then the *Millennium Falcon* shot out a metal hook and caught Vader's TIE fighter. "Got him! Hook, line, and stinker!" cheered Han.

It looked like the rebels were about to win another battle, but before they could reel Darth Vader in, Boba Fett returned.

The *Millennium Falcon* tried to jump into hyperspace

again with the TIE fighter bumbling along behind them.

"It's Vader!" said Leia. "He's too heavy."

"Of course we had to capture the Sith Lord that's ninety percent metal," grumbled Han.

Then Chewbacca had an idea. He pointed out of the front windshield.

"I don't see anything but that same asteroid field," said Han.

Chewbacca threw his hands up in frustration again. He took control of the ship just as Boba Fett moved in front of the *Millennium Falcon* to prepare another attack. The Wookiee waited a moment, then he shifted the starship down just as Fett let out a blast. Quickly, Chewbacca whipped Vader around on the hook like he was fishing, and cast the Dark Lord out toward *Slave I*.

"What are you doing?" screamed Luke, Han, and Leia.

Then the space monster leapt out from its cave again and swallowed both Vader's and Boba Fett's starships whole!

"Whoa," whispered the others, who couldn't believe their eyes.

"Yes! Operation: Later Vader was a success!" cheered Luke. "I bet we'll never see those guys again! Does this mean I get another medal?"

"A medal for underestimating the power of the dark side," Obi-Wan's ghostly voice joked.

"Brrraghhhggg-ha-ha-ha-ha!" Chewbacca boomed with laughter. His voice had finally returned.

"I think fuzzball here earned the medal this time," said Han as he motioned to Chewie. "Now, let's get out of here before those two give that worm a stomachache."

A MOST DANGEROUS DROID

As the *Millennium Falcon* landed unnoticed in Mos Eisley, a lone droid exited the ship. It was C-3PO and he had been sent on a special mission to complete a list of tasks for the Rebel Alliance.

"There was no need to write a list, Master Luke," said C-3PO. "I have committed these requests to

memory. I am a programmable protocol droid, you know."

"The list is to use just in case," said Luke.

"Just in case what?" asked C-3PO.

"In case something goes wrong, you bucket of bolts," answered Han Solo. "Don't forget my shades on that list. These two suns are a double-bright pain on the eyes. And nobody looks cool when they're squinting."

With that, Han and Luke closed the bay door and stayed hidden inside their ship.

"Heard you, I did," said Yoda's ghost, appearing next to the rebels. "Cool, I look always."

"AAAH!" screamed Han and Luke. "Yoda! You cannot keep sneaking up on us like that!"

"Funny, it is, to scare you," snickered Yoda. "Seen the look on your faces, you should have."

"Yuk it up, little Jedi Master," said Han. "To what do we owe this pleasure?"

"*Hmmmm*, warn you, I must," said Yoda. "Bad

feeling, I have, about that droid."

"You and me both," said Han as he watched C-3PO wander into the sandy streets of Mos Eisley. "He can be a magnet for trouble. That's why we're going to keep a close eye on him."

***

"Perhaps I should start with Captain Solo's cool shades first," C-3PO said to himself as he stopped in front of a men's clothing shop. He went inside and found a large selection of sunglasses.

"Oh, my . . . so many options . . . Which would Captain Solo like best?" C-3PO wondered aloud. "I'll have to try each pair on."

And so he did. But as he tried on the different pairs of glasses, another shopper entered. It was the Emperor, and his Imperial Guards escorted him.

"Please, Your Evilness, this is a simple errand that you could have let us handle ourselves," begged one of the guards.

"Oh, and have you return from the best tailor on

Tatooine with a robe that doesn't suit my evil needs?" scoffed the Emperor. "No, thank you. Bah, you Imperial Guards can't choose clothing to save your lives! Look at you, dressed in RED! That's no way to strike fear into the hearts of your enemies. You look like giant red carpets. People are lining up to walk over you! Besides, I look horrible in red."

C-3PO tried to hide, but it was too late. The Emperor had spotted the droid.

"You there," called out the Emperor. "I want to see something in black. And not this deep-space black that's really gray. I want to see black-hole black. I want a robe that makes my white, pale skin really stand out and my yellow eyes glow."

"Y-y-y-y-yes, sir," stuttered a scared C-3PO. "Let me see what we have in the back."

"Great, a nervous, glitchy droid," the Emperor complained. "That's the last thing I need right now. The things I must deal with to look as good as I do for my adoring public."

C-3PO returned with three robes for the Emperor. "Perhaps one of these will work for you?"

"Ugh," objected the Emperor. "These robes are awful! I am not an Ewok, a Jedi, or an astromech droid! And none of these are black, you color-blind misfit. Who built you anyway?"

"Funny story about that—" started C-3PO, but he was not meant to finish.

"Do I look like a clown?" interrupted the Emperor.

"No, sir," said C-3PO.

"Then why do you dress me like one?!" And in a flash, the Emperor sizzled C-3PO with a blast of Force lightning. The poor droid lit up like fireworks, caught in the dark side's jolt.

The Imperial Guards ran over and threw water on C-3PO. "See, sir, this is why we like handling your shopping."

"Forget it," sneered the Emperor. "I heard there's a sale on used death ray parts across town."

The Emperor and his guards left the shop, leaving C-3PO doused and fried.

***

Luckily, Han and Luke were not too far behind C-3PO after Yoda's cryptic warning. They found their friend in the shop, and quickly rushed him back to the medical bay on a secret rebel base on the nearby moon of Chenini.

They burst through the doors and hooked C-3PO up to as many computers as they could find.

"What happened?" cried Leia, who came running in. "Did you send Threepio to pick up your dry cleaning again?"

Han and Luke looked embarrassed. "In our defense, we didn't know the Emperor was going to be on Tatooine."

"Get out of here, both of you," said Leia in her stern voice. "You should just be glad that the entire Empire didn't follow you back here."

BOOM! An explosion shook the base. Han, Luke,

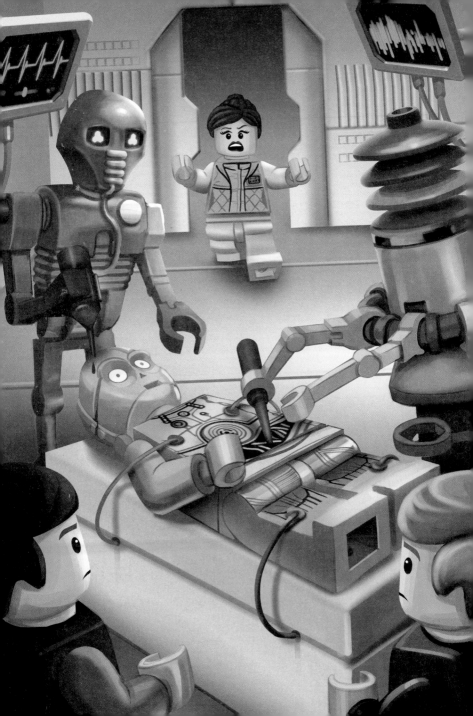

and Leia all stared at one another.

"That was the entire Empire, wasn't it?" asked Leia. "They're here, aren't they?"

Han and Luke shrugged their shoulders guiltily. "Well, it didn't look like the biggest ship in the world following us to the secret base."

"You're lucky the other rebels relocated to our next base this morning," said Leia. "But that means we're going to have to fight the Empire alone."

"Maybe I could get the *Millennium Falcon* in time to serve as a diversion," suggested Han.

"Too late, it is," said Yoda's ghost, who had snuck back into the room.

"AHHHH!" screamed Luke, Han, and Leia. *"STOP DOING THAT!"*

"HA-HA!" chuckled Yoda. "Old, that joke never gets."

"Seriously, Master, now is not the best time," whined Luke. "Our friend is hurt, and the Empire is blasting down our front door."

"*Hmmmm*, but perhaps your friend *is* the answer," announced Yoda in his cryptic way.

Just then, C-3PO started to reboot from his bed. "Oh, Master Luke, Captain Solo! I am afraid I was unable to obtain your requested goods, but I still have the list."

C-3PO held the list in the air and suddenly all the medical equipment flew away from him. Luke, Han, and Leia barely dodged the flying gear. The rebels armed themselves quickly, thinking that the Empire attack had finally reached them.

"That was quite odd," said C-3PO. "As I was saying, here's your list, Captain Solo."

But as C-3PO went to give Han the list, the droid seemed to push Han's blaster and Luke's lightsaber out of their hands.

"How did Threepio get hurt again?" asked Leia.

"Force lightning . . . from the Emperor," puzzled Han. "But these telekinetic powers are almost Jedi-like?"

"Impossible," said Luke. "A droid cannot be a Jedi."

"But I'm not a regular droid any more, sir," said C-3PO with a newfound confidence in his voice. He stared at his hands in amazement. "And I will not be pushed around again!"

C-3PO jumped up and ran toward the sounds of blasting that echoed through the base.

"Wait!" called out his friends, but C-3PO had already leapt into action. A squadron of stormtroopers marched into the hallway and began blasting at the lone droid.

"Oh, so you want to play? I'll show you little bowling pins how See-Threepio rolls!" hollered C-3PO as he raised his hand. Surprisingly, the medical gear gathered into a ball right into the droid's grip, and then C-3PO rolled it like a bowling ball to strike down the stormtroopers.

"Who's next?!" asked C-3PO, almost bragging about his new powers. "Because I AM THE DROID YOU ARE LOOKING FOR!"

Luke, Han, and Leia had never seen anything like

this. Their mild-mannered robot friend had gone from a zero to a hero. He'd saved their lives and possibly the entire Rebel Alliance.

But as the dust settled, a new force entered the room with the familiar machine-breathing that sent a chill down the rebels' backs. It was Darth Vader.

"Have you come to battle me?" called out C-3PO.

"No, silly droid," said Vader. "I've come to finish you."

Both C-3PO and the Sith Lord unleashed a Force-push attack, but there was only one problem: C-3PO's attack didn't work at all. The droid was tossed backward and thudded against a wall.

"Had . . . enough . . . Vader?" C-3PO gasped as he slumped down.

"You think," said Vader as he stepped forward, "that being stung by the Emperor's Force lightning turned you into a Jedi. But really, it just turned you into a glorified magnet. And I am not afraid of magnets. Or droids."

"Ghosts, what about, *hmmmm*?" said Yoda's ghost from behind Darth Vader. "Magnetic personality, you are not."

With Vader distracted by Yoda, C-3PO used the last of his magnetic strength to push Darth Vader. The Sith Lord tripped over the medical gear debris and became tangled up in his own cape.

"HA-HA! Next fall, see you!" shouted Yoda as the others scooped up C-3PO and escaped to the *Millennium Falcon*.

They blasted off, leaving Vader and the invading Empire forces behind. In the end, C-3PO's battles had bought the rebels enough time to slip away safely to fight again another day. Perhaps C-3PO was not the most dangerous droid in the galaxy, but he had come across both the Emperor and Darth Vader and lived to tell the tale.

GLOSSARY

ASTEROID FIELD
A part of space that is occupied by many large, drifting rocks, called asteroids. It is very dangerous for starships to fly into an asteroid field.

ASTROMECH DROID
Special droids that help with navigation and repairing starships.

BLASTER
An energy weapon that is popular in the galaxy. It fires bolts that look like laser beams.

BOBA FETT
Son of bounty hunter, Jango Fett. Boba also becomes a famous bounty hunter over the years.

BOUNTY HUNTER
Someone who tracks and captures wanted persons for payment.

C-3PO
A golden protocol droid, who often acts as translator. He was built by Anakin Skywalker and later serves his son, Luke. He is commonly seen alongside his counterpart, R2-D2.

CHENINI
One of the moons of the desert planet, Tatooine.

CHEWBACCA
Loyal friend of smuggler-turned-rebel, Han Solo. The Wookiee is his co-pilot aboard the *Millennium Falcon*.

CHOPPER
An old and grumpy astromech droid that helps to maintain the rebel freighter, *Ghost*.

DARK LORD
Honorary title of evil Sith, like Darth Vader.

DARK SIDE

The side of the Force that is used for evil deeds. The Sith embrace the dark side of the Force.

DARTH VADER

Apprentice of Darth Sidious, aka the evil Emperor Palpatine. At his master's side he spreads fear and loathing in the Empire. He was once the Jedi, Anakin Skywalker.

DEATH STAR

A huge battle station in space that looks like a little moon. Its superlaser can destroy whole planets.

DROID

Droids are robots built for various purposes in the galaxy.

EMPEROR

Title of the ruler over the Galactic Empire.

EMPIRE

Association of worlds from all over the galaxy that are ruled by self-proclaimed Emperor Palpatine. The Empire rules by fear and violence.

EWOK

Little furry natives of the forest moon of Endor that live in tree-house villages. They look kind of cute, but they are fierce warriors, too.

EZRA BRIDGER

An orphan boy from the rim world, Lothal, who joins a team of rebels. He is strong in the Force and wants to become a Jedi.

GALAXY

Conglomerate of billions of star systems with countless planets.

GHOST

An old space freighter that is modified to be a powerful battle ship for the rebel team of Lothal. She is owned and piloted by Hera Syndulla.

GRAND MOFF

A high-ranking official in Palpatine's Galactic Empire who has authority over military forces and whole regions of the galaxy.

HAN SOLO

A smuggler who joins the Rebel Alliance. Together with his friend Chewbacca, he flies the *Millennium Falcon*.

HERA SYNDULLA

Owner and pilot of the *Ghost*. Together with Kanan Jarrus, she leads a ragtag rebel team that is based on Lothal.

HYPERSPACE

Starships reach hyperspace by flying faster than lightspeed. Through hyperspace they can get from one point of the galaxy to another very quickly.

IMPERIAL GUARDS

An elite unit of the Empire's armed forces that is tasked with the protection of Emperor Palpatine. They wear distinctive red robes and helmets.

INQUISITOR

A sinister agent of Darth Vader who hunts down Jedi. He uses the dark side of the Force and carries a red lightsaber, but he is not a real Sith.

JAWA

The little Jawas live as scavengers in the deserts of Tatooine. They are wily traders and wear dark hooded robes that only show their glowing eyes.

JEDI

Group of followers of the light side of the Force. The Jedi fight for the good cause and are considered to be keepers of peace and justice in the Republic. In the days of the Empire there are only a few of them left.

KANAN JARRUS

A Jedi who escaped Palpatine's Order 66 when he was still a Padawan. He is part of a small rebel cell and trains young Ezra Bridger in the ways of the Force.

LEIA ORGANA

Princess Leia is one of the Rebel Alliance's leaders. Her homeworld, Alderaan, was destroyed by the first Death Star.

LIGHTSABER

A sword with a glowing blade of pure energy that penetrates almost anything. In most cases, Jedi lightsabers have green or blue blades, Sith lightsabers have red ones.

LOTHAL

An Outer Rim planet with large grass plains. When the Empire arrived, they forced many farmers to leave their land and established factories and mines instead. It is home to a small rebel cell.

LUKE SKYWALKER

Hero of the Rebel Alliance who destroyed the first Death Star in his X-wing starfighter. Being Anakin Skywalker's son, he is very strong in the Force and becomes a powerful Jedi.

MILLENNIUM FALCON

An old, patched-up space freighter and—according to its owner, Han Solo—the fastest ship in the galaxy.

MOS EISLEY

City on the desert world Tatooine, with a large spaceport.

OBI-WAN KENOBI

A Jedi Master who fought in the Clone Wars. He trained Anakin Skywalker to become a Jedi, and his son Luke, many years later.

PADAWAN

A young Jedi student who is not yet a fully fledged Jedi Knight.

R2-D2

Brave R2-D2 is an astromech droid that helps with navigation and repairing starships. He undergoes many adventures alongside galactic heroes—often together with his counterpart, C-3PO.

REBEL ALLIANCE

Resistance fighters against the evil Empire who want to restore a democratic Republic. It was formed from various smaller rebel cells like the one based on Lothal.

SABINE WREN

A teenage girl from the planet Mandalore, and explosives expert of the Lothal rebel cell. She wears typical Mandalorian armor, but with a certain artistic flair.

SITH

Evil Force users who have embraced the dark side and who want to have more and more power. They are arch-enemies of the Jedi. For hundreds of years there have only been two of them—a master and an apprentice.

SLAVE I

A heavily armed starship that belongs to bounty hunter, Boba Fett. He inherited it from his father, Jango.

STORMTROOPERS

The soldiers of the Empire. Stormtroopers wear white armor with a closed helmet. This way, their faces cannot be seen and they all look the same.

TATOOINE

A remote rim world with a surface of mostly desert. Besides the native Tusken Raiders and Jawas, there are also settlers from other planets. The criminal, Jabba the Hutt, has his palace here and a popular sport is podracing.

TELEKINETIC POWERS

The ability to move objects with your mind alone.